BIG APPLE BARN™

HOLD YOUR HORSES!

WELCOME TO
BIG APPLE BARN!

BIG APPLE BARN™

HOLD YOUR HORSES!

by **KRISTIN EARHART**

Illustrations by
JOHN STEVEN GURNEY

SCHOLASTIC INC.
New York   Toronto   London   Auckland   Sydney
Mexico City   New Delhi   Hong Kong   Buenos Aires

To Craig, again and always
—K.J.E.

No part of this publication may be reproduced, stored in a retrieval system, or transmitted in any form or by any means, electronic, mechanical, photocopying, recording, or otherwise, without written permission of the publisher. For information regarding permission, write to Scholastic Inc., Attention: Permissions Department, 557 Broadway, New York, NY 10012.

ISBN-13: 978-0-545-03473-9
ISBN-10: 0-545-03473-6

12 11 10 9 8 7 6 5 4 3   8 9 10 11 12 13/0

Printed in the U.S.A.   40
First printing, March 2008

Contents

Chapter One

An Overnight Outing

"Are you sure you want to do this?" Roscoe asked. The mouse was sitting on the top of Happy's stall door, so he could stare right into his friend's deep brown eyes.

"Of course I'm sure," Happy Go Lucky responded with a toss of his glossy black mane. The young pony first looked at Roscoe, then at Prudence, the barn cat. As usual, the mouse was doing most of the talking.

Roscoe sighed. "I don't know. An overnight trail ride? Have you ever done anything like that before? The woods are dark at night. And spooky." The mouse gave himself a little hug and shivered.

Happy was touched by his friend's concern, but he also knew that Roscoe sometimes exaggerated.

"Don't worry. Everything will be fine," the pony said. "The stall door at my old barn was open all the time. I could go outside at night whenever I wanted."

"But you'll be deep in the woods, Happy," Roscoe insisted, shaking his head. "It's not the same."

"I won't be alone. Sassy and Goldi are going," Happy offered, but Roscoe was still scowling. "So is Big Ben. He'll make sure we're all safe. Right, Prudence?" Happy looked to the wise tabby cat for support. He knew she'd see his side of things.

"It's true," Prudence said. "Big Ben is going on the trail ride."

Happy pricked his ears forward, waiting for Prudence to say more, but she never said more than she needed to. Happy didn't think twice when the barn cat raised her eyebrows and walked away.

"Promise you won't worry about me?" Happy asked Roscoe. He watched as the mouse shrugged his shoulders. That's what Roscoe always did when he lost an argument.

They both knew that Big Ben would take charge on the trail ride. Big Ben was a talented show jumper. The tall chestnut horse had traveled all over the country, competing at the top shows with the barn's trainer, Diane Marshall. He had won so many ribbons and trophies that they didn't all fit in the Big Apple Barn display case. Happy believed that the noble jumper could do anything.

"Besides," Happy added with a swish of his tail, "I'm already tacked up. Ivy just went to get her sleepover pack, and then it's time to leave." Ivy Marshall was Diane's younger daughter and Happy's favorite rider. Happy wouldn't want to go on this adventure with anyone else. He knew they'd take good care of each other.

"Fine," Roscoe replied. He raised his nose in the air and looked at the ceiling. "But I think I'll sit this one out."

Happy smiled a little. He remembered

the last time Roscoe had joined a horse-and-pony outing. They had gone to the Spring Festival, and Roscoe had found more than his fair share of trouble there. Happy thought it was probably a good thing that Roscoe wanted to stay home this time. "That's okay," he told the mouse. "I understand if you don't want to go. We'll be back tomorrow afternoon. I'll tell you all about it then."

"Looks like Ivy's on her way now," Roscoe said, pointing at the small girl walking down the barn aisle. "I'd better skedaddle. Be careful in the woods!" Roscoe gave a quick wave, then scampered down the stall door and under the wall.

"Howdy, Happy!" Ivy said with a giggle. "Everyone's just about ready." As she spoke, she opened the door and stepped into Happy's stall. She tickled underneath his chin and kissed his forehead. "Time to buckle my sleeping bag to your saddle." Ivy stepped farther into the stall, making sure to run her hand along Happy's side so he knew exactly where she was. She hummed as she attached her overnight pack to the saddle.

Just then, Happy heard a familiar *clip-clop*. He looked over his stall door. Sure enough, Big Ben was coming down the barn aisle with Diane at his side. The pair paused, and

the trainer smiled at her daughter. "All set, sweetheart?" Diane asked.

Happy smiled up at Big Ben. The horse had warm, brown eyes and a strong jawbone. He stood tall, his head held high, and gave Happy a nod.

Happy responded with a soft nicker. He was excited to be going on a trail ride with his friend. Happy had never been in the woods with the older horse. Big Ben had such good advice about life at Big Apple Barn and horse shows, Happy guessed that he knew a lot about going on trail rides, too.

Two more ponies and their riders lined up behind Big Ben and Diane. "We're all set," Ivy's older sister, Andrea, announced.

Diane glanced at Ivy and Happy, then turned to look at Andrea and the third rider, Nell. "Well, let's get going so we can set up camp before sunset," Diane said.

Diane clicked her tongue, and Big Ben stepped toward the big barn door. Happy snorted as he watched his friend pass. Then Ivy swung open his stall door, and they were on their way!

Chapter Two

Into the Woods

Outside the barn, the summer sun was warm on Happy's brown coat. Steady rain had fallen for almost a week, but now it was sunny — just in time for their big trail ride! Happy raised his head and took a deep breath of fresh air. He stood patiently while Ivy pulled herself into the saddle. Big Ben and the other ponies started toward the path into the woods.

As usual, Ivy's big sister, Andrea, was riding Sassy. Sassy was a stylish appaloosa with a spunky personality. She was a large pony, like Happy, and she was also one of Happy's closest friends.

Nell was matched with Goldi. Nell had started riding lessons at Big Apple Barn over the winter. She and Ivy were the same age and had become fast friends. After Ivy mentioned the sleepover trail ride, Nell had begged her parents to let her go, too. Diane had assured them that, even though Nell was a beginner, she would be safe on Goldi. With her lush blond mane and tail, Goldi was as pretty as she was good-natured. Goldi was much shorter than Happy and Sassy, but she had been a lesson pony for years and they admired her.

"Come on, Happy," Ivy said, leaning forward and patting his neck. "Let's catch up." With a nudge of her heel, Ivy asked Happy to move forward. Happy picked up a trot. Soon he was just behind the others. As they neared the far side of the pasture, they passed a group of horses from Big Apple Barn grazing in the field. The horses lifted their heads and watched Big Ben lead the ponies toward the woods.

"Look, you guys," said a sleek, black horse. "It's the cow ponies hitting the trail." He snickered and the other horses in the pasture did the same.

Sassy rolled her eyes as Happy walked up next to her. "That Cobalt thinks he's so smart," she said.

"I bet he wishes he were going with us," Happy said. He glanced back at the black horse with the arched neck and lightning blaze down his face.

"I don't think so," Sassy replied in a

hushed tone. "He told Dapper Dan that he wanted Diane to take him to a show this weekend. He thinks the trail ride is silly."

"That's crazy," Happy said. "Why would Diane take Cobalt to a show? Big Ben is her show horse."

"Well, she's been riding Cobalt more lately, and he's been jumping really well. Dapper Dan thinks Diane is going to let Ben retire. Then Cobalt will be her show horse."

Happy thought that fiery Cobalt was totally different than reliable Big Ben. With this news in mind, Happy looked at his friend, who was in the front of the group. Ben's chestnut mane shone in the sun. He held his head high as they neared the forest. Happy tried to imagine Big Ben not going to shows, but he couldn't. Showing was what Big Ben did.

"I don't believe it," Happy insisted.

"I don't want to believe it, either," Sassy said with a sigh. "But why would Diane bring Big Ben on this trip? Top show horses don't spend the night in the woods. They need to be careful not to get hurt."

Happy thought about what Sassy had said. She was right. He had never seen Diane take Big Ben on the trails before! She usually rode one of the lesson horses. Why had she changed her mind? Was Big Ben going to retire? Happy couldn't help thinking about all the silver bowls in the trophy case, all the champion ribbons in blue, red, and gold.

"What did Goldi say about this?" Happy asked in a whisper, so the little pony did not overhear him.

"She said that all horses and ponies get older, and that's just the way it is," Sassy said, glancing quickly at Goldi.

"I'm not going to think about it," Happy replied. But as they entered the forest, it was the only thing on his mind. "I'm going to get up closer to the front," he announced finally. He hoped that, if he was closer to Big Ben, he'd feel better.

"Whoa, Happy! What are you doing?" Ivy called out as the brown pony suddenly pulled at the reins and pushed his way past Sassy and Goldi. "I'm sorry!" she said to Andrea and Nell. "That's not like him." Then she leaned forward in the saddle and spoke so only Happy could hear. "Happy, you need to mind your manners. This is a long ride, and we should try to be nice to everyone."

Happy snorted in reply. He wasn't worried about being nice. He was worried about Big Ben.

Chapter Three

A Big Worrywart

At first, Happy did feel better walking right behind Big Ben. Now he could relax and enjoy the outdoors. Happy loved being under the trees, watching slivers of sun shimmer through the leaves.

Diane had a map of the woods, and she had chosen a skinny trail that led straight into the forest. Happy had never been on it before. The path was covered with pine needles and acorns, and looked like it was rarely used. In the distance, Happy could hear running water. It was exciting to be so close to nature — much better than grazing in the pasture!

"How about we sing a camp song?" Diane asked.

"Yeah!" Ivy and Nell answered together.

At first, Andrea grumbled from the back of the line, but she joined in once she heard the chorus, singing the loudest of all.

The ponies walked at a quick pace to keep up with Big Ben's long strides. Happy's mane flopped against his neck as he stepped in rhythm with the girls' melody.

Up ahead, Happy noticed a giant tree with a wide trunk and twisted branches on the edge of the path. Thick green moss grew on its shady side. Happy guessed that the tree was more than a hundred years old.

"Watch your step." Big Ben nickered a warning. "Don't trip on this tree's big roots."

Happy nodded, placing his hooves down carefully. "It's beautiful, isn't it?" he said under his breath.

Big Ben's ear flickered back, and then he turned his head slightly. "It's dangerous. That's what it is." His deep voice echoed under the canopy of leaves.

"Oh. Yeah," Happy said, but the roots did not seem unsafe to him.

"It looks like the leaves up there are wet. They could be slippery," Big Ben advised. "Make sure the others know," he added.

Happy searched the path, but he didn't see any slick patches of leaves. "Look out for wet leaves," Happy announced, just in case. Goldi and Sassy pricked their ears forward, paying attention to the trail.

When they neared a fast-running stream, Diane stopped Big Ben, so he could study the options. The tall horse lowered his head, putting his nose into the water. When he raised it, he turned to look at the ponies. "Everyone should jump this creek," he said. "It's small, but there are sharp rocks on the bottom."

As soon as he had finished talking, Big Ben trotted toward the stream and flew over it with a stylish leap. Happy was excited to jump the water. It was one of the best parts of being in the woods. It was almost as fun as jumping over fallen logs!

Big Ben watched closely as the rest of the ponies made their

way to the other side of the stream, and then he set out again.

Happy quietly followed Big Ben. He decided not to try to chat, since Big Ben was concentrating on the path. Happy felt like he had a lot more fun when he and Ivy went into the woods alone.

Before too long, the group came to a wide clearing.

"Let's take a break," Diane called out to the girls. "I want to check the map, so that we choose the best path."

Since Happy was standing next to Goldi, Ivy and Nell started to talk. The two friends had lots in common, loving horses most of all.

The sun was so bright, Happy blinked several times so his eyes could adjust. Once they did, he spotted a bunch of horses in a grassy meadow nearby. There were several young foals, frolicking and playing tag. Happy noticed that they did not stray far from their mothers. But one foal lifted his nose in the air and looked over at the trail riders. At once, he trotted toward them.

The foal was a deep gray with dapples of white. He lifted his legs through the tall grass, approaching at a fast pace.

"Hey!" he called. He ran right up to the fence and stuck his head over the railing.

"I'm Stormshadow. Stormy for short. Who are you? What are you doing here?"

Happy had to laugh. The foal was curious. And bold.

"We're from Big Apple Barn," Big Ben replied.

The foal stared at Big Ben, waiting for more.

"We're going on an overnight trail ride in the woods," Happy added, when it was clear Big Ben wasn't going to say anything else.

"Oh!" The foal's eyes sparkled. "I've never heard of anyone doing that before. I want to go, too."

Big Ben chuckled. "I'm afraid you're too young."

The foal's head drooped a little. "Well, it sounds like a great quest. It must be so exciting." The foal stared off into the woods. "I want to go on a quest."

"Maybe one day," Happy encouraged. He knew that a sleepover in the forest must sound like terrific fun.

"Oh, that's not likely," Big Ben stated. "You, my young colt, are a Thoroughbred." Big Ben continued in a low voice. "I have Thoroughbred blood, too, which is why I am good in the show ring." Big Ben paused and looked the foal over again. "With your long legs and neck, I'm certain you'll be a racehorse, and a racehorse has no place on these rocky forest trails. You must take really good care of yourself."

The foal looked up to Beg Ben and gave a slight nod, but then his head drooped with disappointment again.

Chapter Four

Hangman's Hollow

Happy was about to say something to cheer up Stormy, when Diane cleared her throat. "Okay, let's head down this hill toward those tall trees over there." Diane motioned with her hand as she called to the group.

"It looks spooky," said Nell.

"Oh, that's no big deal," Andrea said. "It's just some old trees."

"Let's move, everyone," Diane called. "It's getting late."

When Diane tugged on his reins, Big Ben set out without another word to Stormy. The foal looked glum as he watched the show jumper stride away.

Happy frowned. Big Ben had always given him such good advice. He was surprised that the older horse had not been more understanding with Stormy. Happy lingered while the other ponies followed Big Ben. Ivy seemed to know that Happy wasn't ready to go.

Glancing back, Diane called to her younger daughter. "You can stay here for a few minutes, if you want. I know it's fun to canter on the trails. Just don't get too far behind."

Ivy smiled at her mom and then bent forward, so she was close to Happy's ear.

"What do you think, boy? Do you want to stay here a little bit?" she asked, giving Happy a light pat. "You can say good-bye to this little guy."

Happy nickered and leaned his head in close to the foal's. "It's okay, Stormy," Happy said. "You don't have to be a racehorse. Thoroughbreds can do lots of neat things."

"But this is a racehorse farm," Stormy explained. "We are all supposed to run fast and win races when we grow up." The silver hairs in his coat seemed to sparkle in the sun. He pawed at the grass with his front hoof. "I like galloping, but I want to do other stuff, too."

"Don't worry," Happy said. "I'm sure you'll get the chance to do all sorts of things that you like."

Just then, Happy heard a long, shrill whinny. It was Big Ben. He was calling him.

"Come on, Happy," Ivy said. "We don't want to get lost."

"I have to go," Happy explained to the foal. "It was nice to meet you, Stormy."

Ivy clicked her tongue. Then Happy turned and started to canter down the hill, trying to catch up to his friends. He could see Sassy's spotted back disappearing into a cluster of trees. He followed the trail through the tall grass until he reached a small opening to the forest.

Ivy slowed him down as he neared the wooded area. Happy stopped and looked up ahead. The sun was low in the sky, and it was already becoming dark under the trees. The shadows were long. Happy took a deep breath. The air smelled damp. He pricked his ears forward and listened for Big Ben and the other ponies, but he couldn't hear a thing.

"This is it, Happy," Ivy said. "We saw Sassy go in here. They can't be far away."

Happy lifted his head and looked up. He saw the tall trees Diane had pointed to. It was the right trail, but something didn't *feel* right. Happy took a cautious step on the soft path and looked around again. When Ivy gave him a nudge, he took another step. The trees grew closer together, and little sunlight came through the leaves overhead.

"I wonder why they call it Hangman's Hollow," Ivy whispered. The very name gave Happy chills. He thought he could hear the giant old trees creaking as he walked by them.

The path led down a hill. A cool breeze blew here that he had not felt at Big Apple Barn. "We have to go faster, or we'll never catch up," Ivy said.

Happy picked up a trot, flicking his ears

to try to hear anyone else in the woods. Happy didn't know what it was, but he sensed that something was wrong. He was certain he would feel better once they found the others.

"Up there," Ivy called. Happy could hear the relief in her voice. Sure enough, he could see Goldi's blond tail as she turned around a bend in the trail ahead. Happy lengthened his stride, and soon he was right behind his friends.

Nell turned in her saddle as Goldi and Happy kept walking. "I was worried about you," she said to Ivy in a small voice. "Your mom said you were perfectly safe with Happy, and we'd stop and wait if you didn't catch up soon. But I was still worried."

"Thanks," Ivy said. "We're here now." She was trying to sound brave, but Happy knew she had been anxious.

Nell paused and looked at the tree branches arching overhead. "This place is pretty, but it's also kind of creepy."

Ivy nodded. "Happy and I are glad to be back with the group," she confessed. "My mom told me that this trail is the fastest way to get to where we're spending the night. We should be out of these woods before too long."

"That's good to know," Nell said. "We'll be okay, won't we, Goldi?" Goldi kept plodding along the path. The small pony did not scare easily.

Still, Happy believed something wasn't right. His left ear flicked backward when he heard a sharp crack behind him. He couldn't tell what made the noise, but he didn't like the sound of it.

"What is it, boy?" Ivy asked.

Happy gave a short snort.

"It won't be long now," Ivy said, patting his neck.

But it was. They walked along the path for almost an hour. Happy could not tell how far they were from the end of the woods. The path twisted and turned, and the trees grew so close together he could not see through them. He could only just glimpse a swish of Big Ben's tail before the horse went around another curve in the trail.

An owl hooted from a branch high above, and Happy knew it was getting late. Then, all of a sudden, Goldi stopped.

"What's going on?" Happy whispered to the caramel-colored pony.

"I don't know," she said. "Sassy stopped, and so did Big Ben."

"Okay, everyone!" came Diane's voice. "There's a small clearing here. Let's all gather around."

The riders looked at one another as they steered their ponies into a small area without trees. There, Happy saw why they had stopped. A gigantic pine tree had fallen across the trail, and there was no way to get past it!

"Well, I'm afraid we can't go any farther today," Diane announced. "It's too dark to find a safe way around this tree." Diane had dismounted and was now standing next to the oversized trunk. She gave the tree an affectionate pat. "It's too bad, because Forget-me-not Field is not far away. That's where I had planned to set up camp. But we'll have to do it here, in this clearing. Then we'll find a new path tomorrow morning."

"We're sleeping here?" Ivy asked, looking around the dark forest.

Nell swallowed hard.

The owl hooted again, and Happy heard another twig snap. He knew he wouldn't be getting much sleep that night.

Chapter Five

A Ghost Story

Andrea and Diane started a small campfire to cook dinner while Ivy and Nell took care of the ponies. First, the younger girls carried buckets to a nearby stream and brought back water, so Big Ben and the ponies had enough to drink. Then they pulled the grain from Diane's travel pack.

"Sorry we don't have any hay," Ivy said. She poured out half a coffee can of the dried corn in front of Happy and gave him a long pat. "We were supposed to be staying in an open field tonight. You could have eaten as much grass as you wanted. I hope you won't get too hungry." Happy scuffed his hooves on the ground. They touched only dirt and pine needles. Once Happy's small pile of grain was gone, he'd have nothing else to eat.

Ivy apologized to Big Ben and the other ponies, too. They had all worked hard. Happy knew that she wanted to tell them that they had done a good job, but he also knew that words couldn't fill their growling bellies.

Nell tied up the grain bag and put it with the saddles under the old pine tree. Then the two girls found the grooming kit and checked Big Ben and the ponies for any burrs or cuts. Finally, Ivy misted them with

bug spray. She paid special attention to their legs. Then she poured some of the bug spray on a cloth and wiped off their faces and ears.

"Now we should tie them up, just to be safe," Ivy advised. She handed Nell two lead lines and showed her how to tie a knot that they could release quickly if the ponies became scared. "This tree limb is strong," Ivy said, pulling against it.

While the girls were looping Sassy and Goldi's leads over the sturdy branch, Happy asked Big Ben why the girls didn't just let them roam around the clearing. "We don't need to be tied up. They know we would never run away," Happy insisted.

"They are being thoughtful," Big Ben explained. "If something happened, and we were scared, we might want to run. That's how horses react to danger, and it wouldn't be safe for us to race through the woods at night. We'd get hurt."

Happy nodded.

As Ivy attached the lead to Happy's red halter, Happy stared into the black night. The forest looked endless. Happy could only see shadows — and hear the scampering and slithering of animals in the darkness.

"I hope you all sleep tight," Ivy said, waving to Big Ben and the ponies.

"Don't let the bedbugs bite," Nell added with a laugh. Then both girls joined Andrea by the campfire.

Meanwhile, Diane had been studying the map of the forest. She wanted to figure out the quickest way to Forget-me-not Field. They needed to cross that field before they could find the county fairgrounds, where Mr. Marshall would meet them with the trailer the next day.

As the riders gathered around the campfire for dinner, the horses stood at the other end of the clearing. "Well, this place sure is different than spending a night at Big Apple Barn," Big Ben said. "I know Ivy did her best, but the bugs here are nipping me from my head to my hooves."

Happy hadn't noticed any bug bites, but he had thick skin. The bugs never seemed to like him much. Big Ben and the other horses that didn't spend much time outside always felt every little nibble. "Let's stand next to one another, head to tail. That way, we can swat more of them away," Happy suggested. It was what he and his mother used to do back at Shoemaker Stables when the bugs were especially pesky.

Happy backed up, so his tail was next to Big Ben's neck. He began to swish his tail, giving it a lot of swing.

"How we're supposed to sleep out here in the open, I will never know," Big Ben said under his breath. "Even the small stalls at shows are better than this!"

Happy looked around. He thought the trees gave them lots of shelter, and he liked the fresh air. But Big Ben was a barn horse — and a show horse. He wasn't used to trails with uneven ground or streams with stones at the bottom. And he definitely was not used to sleeping outside.

"I've got a story," the horses heard Andrea say as she put a marshmallow on a pointy stick and thrust it into the fire. "It's about why this place is called Hangman's Hollow."

"Andrea, you can't know that!" Ivy insisted. "Don't just make something up to scare us." She watched with wide eyes as the shadows from the campfire played across her older sister's face.

Happy swallowed. He wasn't sure he wanted to hear Andrea's story, either.

"You don't have to listen or believe what I say," Andrea said. "But you won't be able to help yourself." She smiled at Nell, who bit her lower lip.

"Be easy on your little sister and Nell," Diane advised in a kind voice.

"It's just a story," Andrea said with raised eyebrows.

But before she could say more, a creaking moan echoed through the forest, followed by the sound of footsteps on the dry leaves. Diane grabbed her flashlight and swung it in the direction of the sound. The beam bounced off tree limbs and leaves. It lit ferns and moss. But it did not reveal what had made the sound.

Happy saw that the grin had left Andrea's face, which was now ghostly white.

"It's just the woods," Diane said. "The wind can make funny noises in the leaves. But let's not tell any spooky stories tonight, so we can all get some sleep. Besides, it's already past your bedtime, girls."

Diane tucked the three young riders into their sleeping bags and then sat with her back against a nearby tree, so she could see all of them.

Happy stood between Big Ben and Goldi, and though neither of them talked, he was certain they didn't sleep, either. Even calm, collected Goldi was on guard. Happy knew it was a horse's habit to keep watch in the night. It came from when horses had lived together in the wild and needed to protect

themselves from other animals. Horses and ponies usually slept standing up, so they could make a fast escape.

Happy closed his eyes from time to time during the night. But each time he took a peek around, he saw Big Ben with his eyes wide open, ears flicking forward and back. Nothing would happen on his watch.

Chapter Six

Blindman's Bluff

The morning sun glinted through the leaves, giving the campers hope when they woke up. After breakfast, they went over to investigate the tree that had fallen across their path. It was a giant pine that still had all of its branches. The thick trunk was right in the middle of the trail. The roots had been ripped out of the ground. Diane paced from one end of the tree to the other. Ferns and trees grew on all sides. There wasn't any room to get around.

"Do you think we could jump it?" Andrea asked.

Diane shook her head. "It's too risky," she said.

Big Ben overheard Andrea and shook his head, too. "It *is* too risky," he said to the ponies. "The ground is uneven. It would be too hard to land safely. And it is a high jump, even for me."

"Maybe we could get the horses to push the tree out of the way," Nell suggested.

Diane shook her head.

"What does she think we are, draft horses?" Big Ben grunted.

Happy looked at Big Ben out of the corner

45

of his eye. *Nell was just trying to help,* Happy thought. Big Ben had not been himself since the start of the trail ride. Happy hoped they would get home soon, and Big Ben would go back to being the kind, noble horse he admired so much.

Diane ran her hand through her hair. "We'll have to go around," she announced, unfolding the map again. "It's a shame. We were so close, but we'll backtrack for a while. Then we'll head up Blindman's Bluff. From there, we have to cross a little stream, and we'll be in Forget-me-not Field." She traced the way along the map with her finger. "Then we're almost to the fairgrounds."

Andrea and Ivy peered at the map over their mother's shoulder. "It looks long," Ivy said in a small voice. "Maybe we should just go back the way we came."

"What?" Andrea asked. "And miss riding along a hillside trail called Blindman's Bluff?"

When Nell winced at the sound of the trail's name, Diane put a hand on the youngest girl's shoulder. "It'll be fine," she said confidently. "It would take us even longer to turn around and go back to Big Apple Barn. Besides, it's an adventure. So let's pack up, saddle up, and head on out!" Diane pumped her arm to show her excitement. Andrea grinned, but Nell gave Ivy a worried glance.

Sassy put her nose up to Happy's ear. "I know Diane wants us to think it's an easy trip, but I have a funny feeling about this."

Happy looked Sassy in the eye. Sassy cocked her head to one side and sighed. Happy had been so excited about this trail ride, but right now, it didn't seem like much fun. Happy suddenly remembered Stormy, and how the colt had thought their overnight outing sounded like a jolly quest. *If only he were here now,* Happy thought, *he might change his mind.*

With Big Ben in the lead again, the group marched through the forest toward Blindman's Bluff. As the ponies started up the narrow trail along the ridge, it became colder. The trail was slippery from the recent rain. It had not been as muddy in the woods, where the trees had shielded the ground from steady showers.

Sassy was behind Big Ben, followed by Goldi, with Happy at the back. Ivy leaned forward in the saddle to make the climb easier for Happy. He could feel the wet path squish under his hooves. When Happy looked up, he saw a fluffy mist clinging to the mountain. "How are we supposed to see where we're going?" he asked. "There's fog everywhere."

"You just have to trust your hooves. Then you'll know where it's safe," Goldi answered.

"I've been on this trail before. It's a lot of fun when it's not wet and there isn't any fog."

Happy sighed. He usually found the small pony to be reassuring, but not this time. The fog seemed to float in front of his eyes. He tried to remember to let his hooves find the trail, but he stumbled several times. His hooves were filled with mud, and he couldn't keep his footing.

Happy did his best to concentrate. All the while, he kept hearing noises on the trail behind him. He turned to look from time to time, but he couldn't see anything through the mist. *Some quest,* he thought to himself.

"I have a story," Andrea called out. "It's about how this path got the name Blindman's Bluff." She paused before saying, "Just look down!"

Happy glanced down and gulped. The trail was not much wider than he was, and the edge of the mountain just dropped off. Through the patches of fog, Happy could see treetops far below. He gulped again.

"Andrea, that's uncalled for," Diane said. This time her voice sounded tense. "Girls, keep your eyes on the trail. And hold your hands still, so your ponies can feel your support on the reins."

"It's okay, Happy," Ivy soothed. "You're doing great."

Finally, the path began to slope downhill. Now the ponies had to be even more careful. The riders all leaned back in the saddle, to help the horses keep their balance. Happy put his weight on his back legs, so he wouldn't skid forward.

"I think I hear water," Diane announced to boost everyone's spirits. Once they crossed the brook, they would be in Forget-me-not Field, just a step away from the fairgrounds. They were almost home!

Chapter Seven

Babbling Brook

At the foot of the mountain, Happy could hear the ripple of the brook more clearly. He knew they must be close, yet he could not see the water. Even though the mist had lifted, they were still in the woods. Happy saw trees and little else!

Big Ben and the ponies plodded on. Big Ben no longer called out warnings along the trail. Sassy did not make clever comments. They were all worn out and ready to go home.

As he followed Goldi, Happy thought about the moment when he would trot across the stream and sink his head in the lush grass of Forget-me-not Field. It seemed like a long time since he had eaten his morning grain. It had been smaller than his usual breakfast. An animal had gotten into the feed bag in the middle of the night and eaten some of the grain. No one had seen it happen, not even Big Ben.

Now Happy was hungry, and so caught up in his daydream that he didn't pay attention to the leaves rustling behind him.

"There's light ahead!" Diane called. "We're coming out of the forest."

Happy looked up, and saw Big Ben start to trot. The whole line of ponies sped up. Happy could hear the jingle of their bridles.

He shook his mane and lifted his hooves. It was good to have some spring back in his step.

But when Happy joined the others just outside the woods, he gasped. They were standing on the bank of the brook. But it was the widest brook Happy had ever seen. It looked like a river!

"Look how fast it's moving," Ivy said, holding Happy's reins tight.

"It looks deep," Nell commented, biting her lip. Everyone nodded.

"It's not a babbling brook. It's a raging river!" Andrea announced. "What do we do now?"

Big Ben raised his head and pricked his ears. Then he turned, glancing back at the woods. He snorted and stamped his foot. Happy guessed he was thinking about going back.

Diane got out of the saddle. She patted Ben before she walked upstream. After a short while, she came back and headed downstream. Happy knew she was hunting for a safe place to cross. Finally, she returned to the group.

"Let's test the waters," she said when she reached them. Diane slogged down the bank of the stream. It was slippery with mud and fringed with cattails. She held her arms out to keep her balance. On the shore she found a long, skinny branch, which she thrust into the running water. It hit the bottom and stuck straight up.

"It looks like it's a little more than two feet deep," Diane called out before letting go. The branch disappeared under a swell of water. "The stream is wide here, but it's not as fast as the other points. There is a natural dam up that way, but it will be too deep up there. That dam is holding a lot of water back. This is where we have to cross."

No one responded.

"This is our best bet," Diane continued. "We can't turn back. It's too far, and Blindman's Bluff is too steep to climb two times in one day. Besides, we can't camp another night. We don't have enough food." She sighed and looked at the girls. "So, let's go for a swim! Big Ben and I will cross first. The ponies are strong. They can all do this. So can you."

Happy watched the stream as it churned and gushed outside of its banks. He believed he could make it across, but he wished he could be sure. He was going to be carrying Ivy. He couldn't mess up.

Diane walked over to Ivy and Happy. Andrea, Sassy, Nell, and Goldi were standing close by.

"I know this has been harder than we had planned," the trainer confessed to her daughters. "But we're all in this together, and we're all going to be fine." She gave them a reassuring smile. "Happy and Sassy should be able to walk across, but just in case, remember that horses instinctively know how to swim. You just keep them heading toward the other side, and they'll take care of the rest."

Diane turned to Nell. "Nell, Goldi is not as tall as the others. This might be harder for her, since the waves will reach above

her legs. How about you ride with me on Big Ben?"

"Okay," Nell said, sounding shy.

"Goldi is smart and sure-footed. She can make it across on her own. We'll let her follow us," Diane explained. Nell nodded, then took her feet out of the stirrups and jumped to the ground. Diane lifted Nell to the front of Big Ben's saddle.

Diane gave Andrea a thumbs-up and lifted her foot to Big Ben's stirrup, but then she stopped. She turned to Ivy and Happy. "Ivy, you okay?" she asked.

"The stream looks pretty big," Ivy said. "But I know Happy can do it. We'll be fine, Mom."

Diane walked over and gave her daughter a hug. "I know you will," she said. "You'll take care of each other."

Meanwhile, Big Ben had not been able to take his eyes off the stream. He had not said a word since leaving the woods. "I'm not sure about this, Happy," he said suddenly, looking back at the younger pony. "Maybe we should turn around. We don't know what's at the bottom of that stream. Diane depends on me. How can I be sure that I won't let her down?"

Before Happy could think of what to say, Diane had pulled herself into Big Ben's saddle, right behind Nell. When Diane gave him the sign, Big Ben took a deep breath and headed down the stream's slippery shore.

Chapter Eight

Getting Your Hooves Wet

Diane held Big Ben's reins in one hand, and wrapped the other around Nell's waist. Nell held on to Big Ben's chestnut mane.

"Here we go," Diane called, clicking her tongue. Nell bit her lip as the tall horse took short, sturdy strides into the wet bank. His hooves sank in the stiff mud. They made a gurgling sound each time he lifted his legs. Soon he was knee-deep in the rushing water.

Big Ben's strong legs sliced through the stream. Happy watched as the horse went straight across the rough waters, steady all the way. Each step looked sure, and Big Ben climbed up the shore on the other side without a pause.

Diane gave her show horse a long pat, squeezed Nell's shoulders, and leaped out of the saddle.

"Okay, Goldi," Diane said, motioning with her arms from the far bank. The caramel-colored pony moved forward with dainty, cautious steps. She still wore her saddle, but the stirrups were crossed over the top of it, so they would not hit her belly. She placed her front hooves in the brook and, almost at once, a wave washed over her back. With her hind legs, Goldi plunged into the current. She whinnied and lifted her head high to keep it out of the water.

Happy could see only her head and neck, but he could tell that Goldi's legs were working hard beneath her, beating through the water. Her hooves did not reach the bottom. She was swimming.

Happy held his breath. He knew he was much taller than Goldi, so he could probably walk across the stream. But Happy had never swum before, and he was nervous. He was amazed by Goldi's willing attitude.

"Come on, girl," Diane encouraged. With her head raised and ears back, Goldi was almost across. Diane grasped for the pony's bridle and helped her find her footing. Goldi struggled onto the shore and gave herself a long shake, droplets sprinkling from her coat. Diane playfully tousled her mane. "Good work, Goldi," she cheered.

Happy saw Diane say something to Nell, who quickly slid down from Big Ben's saddle and hurried to Goldi's side. The girl collapsed onto the pony's neck and gave her a big squeeze. Finally, she led Goldi to a patch of tender, green grass nearby.

"Okay, Ivy and Happy. It's your turn now," Diane yelled above the sound of churning water.

Ivy swallowed. Happy took a deep breath. He might not have to swim, but the crossing would be hard. He would have to be brave and strong.

"We can do this, Happy. Let's be careful and not rush," Ivy said. "I'll be right here."

Happy trusted Ivy. On hearing her words, he stepped forward, his hoof sliding in the mud as he went down the bank. Then he thrust his legs into the stream. It was cold! He didn't like how slick the bottom was, and he felt unsure of his footing. The water swirled to the top of his legs. He could feel it skim under his belly.

Ivy looked across the rushing water at her mother. Happy reminded himself to take one step at a time. He made sure one hoof was secure on the bottom of the stream before lifting the next.

When he was about halfway across, Happy noticed clusters of twigs floating by in the swells of water. Then he heard a scraping sound. He looked upstream and saw even more twigs. Farther up the brook, large branches were coming loose from the dam.

"Mom?" Ivy called nervously, glancing up the stream.

"You're okay, Ivy," Diane said quickly and evenly. "The dam is holding for now. You keep Happy coming. Stay steady and straight."

Then she raised her chin and called across the stream. "Andrea, dear," Diane continued. "You come ahead. Bring Sassy right across and keep an eye on that dam."

Happy glanced back and saw Andrea nod. Sassy plunged into the stream, her ears pricked forward. She lifted her legs high, splashing along.

Happy looked up to see how much farther he had to go. On the other side, he saw Big Ben standing behind Diane, watching.

They still looked so far away. Then Big Ben gave a nod and whinnied — a long, encouraging whinny.

Happy could feel Ivy's hands firm on the reins. He didn't rush. One step at a time, he neared the other side. Bigger groups of sticks rushed by, and the current seemed to grow stronger. Happy struggled to move his legs against the water. He was exhausted, and the stream was strong. But with another stride, he was climbing the bank.

Ivy reached down and hugged Happy as he came onto even ground. "Good job, Happy!" She sighed in relief. Happy trudged up to Big Ben on weak knees. The horse welcomed him with a nicker. Then Happy turned to watch Sassy.

Out of the corner of his eye, Happy saw a flash of movement from upstream. Water surged through the broken dam. At once, the stream rose. A current crashed over Sassy. Andrea ducked her head and held her breath.

But then Sassy found her footing and lifted herself from the water. The stream raced by, flooded with jagged branches and twigs. They had made it just in time.

Chapter Nine

Forget-me-not Field

The horses grazed on the lush grass of Forget-me-not Field. Everyone needed a break before heading to the final trail, the one that led to the fairgrounds where they were meeting Mr. Marshall. They were relieved that they had all made it across the stream safely. They had been lucky.

At first, Happy had been too tired to eat, but his hunger quickly returned when he tasted the sweet grass. The shady field was dappled with tiny blue forget-me-not flowers. Tall maple trees surrounded the clearing. Diane and the young riders sat on the ground. Ivy was lying back, looking at the clear blue sky. They all were enjoying the calm and quiet.

After a while, Happy paused to take a deep breath. Big Ben did the same.

"You know," the show jumper said, "I can almost smell the fairgrounds from here. I have such great memories there. I'm sure we're close." Big Ben looked beyond the field. After a while, he stamped his foot. "It will be good to be back at Big Apple Barn. I'm glad that things will be back to normal. We should get moving soon."

Happy was wondering if things *would* go back to normal for Big Ben. Would he still be the top show horse when they returned to Big Apple Barn?

"It's funny," Happy said quietly, thinking. "That little foal was right. This was kind of like a quest." The brown pony lowered his head and went back to eating.

Big Ben looked at Happy. "What did you say?"

Happy was busy chewing. "That little foal," he repeated. "Stormy. He said our trip was like a quest."

"That's what I thought you said." Big Ben gave a nod. "Remember how much he wanted to come?" the big horse asked absentmindedly. Then he cocked his head to one side and twitched his ear toward the stream. His ear twitched again. They could still hear the rush of the wild brook that had broken through the dam.

"Oh, no," Big Ben said under his breath. Happy didn't understand. What was wrong?

At once, the horse bounded back toward the rushing waters. He galloped at full speed over the uneven ground. He did not look back when Happy whinnied or Diane called. Big Ben ran as if his life depended on it.

At first, Happy just watched Big Ben go. Then a haunting feeling crept into his heart. It made Happy follow Big Ben right back to the stream as fast as his weary legs would carry him.

When he got there, Happy shivered at the sight. Big Ben was heading back into the brook. The horse's back legs buckled as he slid down the bank. As he scrambled, he fell forward on his knees. But the show jumper forged right into the stream. The water was now up to his chest.

There, at the center of the brook, Happy saw Stormy. The dappled foal was upstream from Big Ben, and he was fighting the powerful current. Happy could barely see the foal's ears and nose above the water.

Happy gasped as Stormy's head bobbed under. Happy closed his eyes, unable to watch. When he opened them, he saw that Big Ben had turned around. The horse was struggling back toward the shore.

There was a lump in Happy's throat. What was Big Ben doing? Had he given up?

Just then, Happy saw Stormy's gray ears pricked forward as the foal swam next to Big Ben. Big Ben inched toward the bank, talking to the foal between heavy breaths. The water rushed past them with gushing speed, but Big Ben's body blocked Stormy from being carried away by the current.

The other ponies, Diane, and the girls were all running toward them now. They arrived just in time to see Big Ben nudge the foal up to the bank. Stormy's front legs were spread out on the muddy ground, his hind legs still fumbling in the water. Diane leaned over and wrapped her arms around Stormy's middle. She picked him up and carried him to the dry grass, the foal's nostrils still flaring. His small body trembled.

"Is this the same foal that we saw yesterday?" Diane asked in disbelief.

"Yeah," Ivy said. "He must have followed us all this way."

Andrea shook her head. "Well, this little guy is amazing, if he did that."

"He made it through Hangman's Hollow in the dark?" Nell questioned.

"And climbed Blindman's Bluff in the fog," Andrea added.

"He's pretty special," Ivy said, running her hand along the foal's wet neck.

"He's not the only one," Diane said. She looked at Big Ben and smiled.

Chapter Ten

A Quest Completed

Once the girls had dried off Stormy, Diane suggested they let him eat grass and regain some energy. As he nibbled at the blades, the ponies asked him all about his outing. The foal told them that he had slid under a broken railing in the pasture fence and then followed Happy's trail into the woods.

"Weren't you scared in Hangman's Hollow?" Happy asked, remembering the creaky trees.

"Yeah, but I knew you all were close. Nothing bad would happen with Big Ben around." Stormy looked admiringly at the older horse, who was grazing nearby.

"Didn't you get hungry?" Goldi wondered.

The foal gave an embarrassed look around the circle of ponies. "Well, yes. But I kind of stole a few bites of your grain."

Happy's jaw dropped. Stormy was the wild animal that had gotten into their feed bag? He guessed he couldn't blame him. There had not been much else to eat in the woods.

Sassy eyed the foal suspiciously. "Why did you stay in the fog and shadows, so we couldn't see you?"

Stormy kept his head down, chewing.

"Well?" Sassy prompted.

"I was afraid you would make me go

78

home," the dappled foal mumbled. His eyelids began to flutter and droop.

Sassy's ears were pricked forward, but before she could ask another question, Ivy walked up holding a saddle.

"Mom says it's time to get going," Ivy said, placing the saddle on Happy's back. "The fairgrounds are just over that way."

Everyone was ready to head home. Diane and Andrea lifted the drowsy foal onto Big Ben's shoulders. Stormy's front legs dangled on one side of the show horse's neck, his hind legs on the other.

Diane sat just behind Stormy in the saddle. As the group crossed Forget-me-not Field and entered the trail to the fairgrounds, the foal fell asleep to the gentle *clip-clop* of Big Ben's hooves.

Happy took his place bchind Big Ben

again. He noticed that Big Ben's knees were scraped and his legs scratched. Happy knew that the cuts were from his second trip into the stream, but Big Ben had not said a word. The horse quietly led the group along the path.

When all of the ponies stepped out of the trees and onto the grassy fairgrounds, Happy spotted Mr. Marshall immediately. "You're a little later than you thought," he said, hurrying over to Diane. "I was getting worried."

Diane just smiled and gestured to Stormy. "Well, we have an extra stop to make on the way home." Mr. Marshall looked wide-eyed at Stormy, still stretched across Big Ben. Slowly, the foal began to stir.

Mr. Marshall helped Diane lift him back to the ground, and then Diane stepped away to call the Thoroughbred stable. She wanted to let them know that their foal was safe.

Stormy wobbled to his legs. He blinked and looked around.

"We're about to get on a trailer, so we can all go home," Happy explained to the foal.

To Happy's surprise, Stormy shook his fluffy black mane and pouted. "But I don't want to go home," he said. "I ran away."

"Stormy, you have a very nice home," Big Ben answered, giving the foal a long, serious look. He seemed to know there was something else on the foal's mind.

"But I'll have to be a racehorse! What if I don't want to be a racehorse?" Stormy asked. "I want to have adventures, instead."

"Oh," Big Ben remarked, "that's what this is about." He took a breath and puckered his lower lip, thinking. "Okay, little guy. Let me see if I can explain this. You are a

Thoroughbred, which means you will probably be strong and fast, so you might be a racehorse or jumper." Big Ben paused.

The ponies were all listening closely to Big Ben, but they tried to pretend they were busy grazing, as their riders took off their saddles for the trailer ride home. Stormy listened closely, too.

"But a horse can do lots of different things in life. I have been a show jumper since I wasn't much older than you. I loved it." Big Ben gave a quick nod. "Now I'm getting older, and I don't show quite as much, so I'm learning new things." He sighed. "I've never done anything like go on a trail ride. It was kind of scary to do something new, but I think I can get the hang of it." Big Ben looked at Happy and gave him a wink.

Stormy blinked several times. "So, I might start out as a racehorse, but then I can try

something else?" He looked at Big Ben hopefully.

"Of course. But what you really need to know," Big Ben said, lowering his head close to Stormy's, "is that a horse is only truly good at what he loves. So find something you love. Will you remember that?"

Stormy blinked, then nodded.

"Good." Big Ben swished his tail and took a deep breath.

Happy and the other ponies exchanged smiles.

Just then, Mr. Marshall and Diane returned to the group. Mr. Marshall looped a lead around Stormy's neck before walking him to the trailer.

"We have good memories at these fairgrounds, don't we?" Diane said as she walked up to Big Ben. She patted the horse's neck. "Of all the wonderful things you've done here, and of all the trophies you've won," she went on, "you have never made me prouder than I am today."

Diane reached her arm around Big Ben's strong neck and buried her face in his silky mane. "You might not be a trail horse, but I can trust you," Diane said softly. "That's why I brought you into the woods. I knew I could trust you, and you proved me right. Thank you, Ben." She gave her horse a hug.

When she pulled away, she realized that Nell and her daughters were watching her. Happy, Sassy, and Goldi had been watching, too.

Big Ben nuzzled Diane's red hair and let out a contented sigh. Happy could tell that, more than anything, Big Ben loved being Diane's horse.

"Well, it's been an adventure," Diane said, smiling at them all. "But how about we head home?"

As much as Happy was looking forward to being back in his comfortable stall and seeing Roscoe and Prudence, he was sad that the overnight trail ride was almost over.

Diane, Mr. Marshall, and the girls loaded Big Ben and the ponies into the trailer. Big Ben whinnied at Diane as she lifted the trailer ramp. Then the horse looked at Happy, Sassy, and Goldi. "So, when do you think we'll hit the trails again?" he asked.

Happy nickered at his friend. Even though the talented jumper might retire from the show ring one day, he knew that Big Ben would always be the top horse at Big Apple Barn.

Glossary
Ponies are Pals (Horses, Too)

Horses are social animals, which means they like to play and live together. In the wild, they live in a group called a herd. Each herd includes smaller groups. Most are made up of a stallion (a male horse), several mares (female horses), and their foals and yearlings. The stallion looks out for and protects the members of its herd.

Because a foal has to be able to escape danger, it is able to walk much sooner than a human baby. A foal should be able to stand up and nurse from its mother when it is only a few hours old. Foals are born in the early spring, and they stay with their mothers for up to two years.

A fairy for every day!

The seven Rainbow Fairies are missing! Help rescue the fairies and bring the sparkle back to Fairyland.

When mean Jack Frost steals the Weather Fairies' magical feathers, the weather turns wacky. It's up to the Weather Fairies to fix it!

Jack Frost is causing trouble in Fairyland again! This time he's stolen the seven crown jewels. Without them, the magic in Fairyland is fading fast!

SCHOLASTIC
www.scholastic.com

FAIRY1